PREDATORS!

Written by Kenn Goin

Illustrated by Patrick Gnan

Reviewed by Frank Indiviglio, Zoologist

Learning Horizons®

AN AMERICAN GREETINGS COMPANY

Manufactured for Learning Horizons, Inc.
One American Road, Cleveland, OH 44144. Printed in China.
Fabriqué pour Learning Horizons, Inc.
One American Road, Cleveland, OH 44144.
Fabriqué en Chine.
Cover & interior design © 2001 Learning Horizons, Inc.

Visit us at: www.learninghorizons.com

It's almost sundown. She slips off the tree branch and silently begins to hunt, just the way she'd learned from her mother. What will she find tonight? And who is she?

A **predator** is any animal that hunts and kills other animals for food.

"THE GHOST OF THE FOREST"

—that's what the black panther is called! She stalks her prey so quietly that it never even realizes the danger until it's too late...until she pounces and it feels her powerful jaws.

Hunted animals are called **prey**.

 **Stats**

size: 75-160 pounds
preferred prey: small to medium size mammals, birds, snakes
attack style: stalk and pounce
hunts: early morning and evening
works: alone

In one leap, this cunning predator can cover 25 feet (7.6 m). She can jump 12 feet (3.6 m) high! And like all leopards, she sees in the dark, hearing the slightest sound. But she is not the only predator on this wild earth. There are many...

such as the **TIGER**, the largest of all cats. When attacking
his prey, he uses his great weight to knock the animal off-
balance. Then he bites down on the animal's throat...and
holds—until it suffocates. At last, he feeds. Tigers often eat
33-40 pounds (15-18 kg) of meat per day!

RUSSIA

Pacific
Ocean

Indian Ocean

These cats are so strong that they can drag the body of a
500 pound (230 kg) animal as far as 1/4 mile (.4 km).

MAN'S BEST FRIEND?

Among the most successful predators on earth are members of the dog family—wolves, foxes, coyotes, jackals, and domestic dogs. In fact, the domestic dog has been humankind's favorite hunting partner for thousands of years.

HUNTING GROUNDS

AFRICA

Atlantic Ocean

Indian Ocean

Like others in this group, African wild dogs often hunt together as a **PACK**. They chase their prey until it is exhausted, and then they bring it down—quickly tearing open the animal's underside.

Stats

size: 44-79 pounds (20-36 kg)
preferred prey: impala, puku, gazelles, wildebeest, zebra
attack strategy: chase to exhaust; rip open
hunts: daytime
works: in packs

SO LOVABLE...

Not all predators are large or seem scary to us. But don't let size fool you. Sea otters, for example, have strong forearms (care to arm wrestle?), paws that can grasp and dig, and they're smart!

Sea otters eat 25% of their body weight in food each day. That's like an adult human eating over 100 sandwiches every 24 hours!

HUNTING GROUNDS

RUSSIA

Alaska

CANADA

Pacific Ocean

UNITED STATES

They hunt in the sea—digging in the muddy ocean floor for clams and other shellfish. Otters use rocks to break open some of the shells; others, they simply crush with their strong teeth and jaws (don't try that at home!).

LET'S MAMBA

When it sees something it wants to eat, the black mamba races after it, quickly strikes to inject venom through its hollow teeth, called FANGS, and then opens its jaws to swallow its victim whole. The snake's venom is so powerful that two full drops are usually fatal for a person—much less kills the small animals that it hunts!

Stats

size: 8-9 feet (2.4 m); up to 14 feet (4.2 m)
preferred prey: small mammals, such as rats, mice and squirrels
attack strategy: chase and inject venom
hunts: day
works: alone

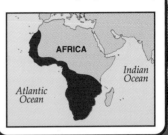

AFRICA

Indian
Ocean

Atlantic
Ocean

All snakes are predators—some inject poisonous venom, while others squeeze their victims to death. And unlike mammals, they instinctively know how to hunt: they don't learn their skills from mom and dad.

IS THAT A TWIG?

Some of the hungriest predators are very small.
Praying mantises, for example, are usually little
bigger than a grasshopper—although in the jungle,
some are nearly 12 inches (.3 cm) long. One kind of
mantis was brought into the United States as a
"garden predator," to help farmers and gardeners
by eating insects that devour plants!

 **Stats**

size: 2-4 inches (5-10 cm) in US
preferred prey: insects and
mites; large species will eat frogs
and lizards
attack strategy: grab and eat
hunts: day
works: alone

A female praying mantis sometimes bites the head off the male during mating!

The praying mantis does not usually chase its prey. It waits until an insect comes within reach, grabs it, and then bites its neck, which paralyzes the victim. Mantises always start eating their victims head-first while they're still alive.

ARACHNOPHOBIA

Spiders and scorpions are called ARACHNIDS by scientists…and they both inject venom to kill. Most spiders wait for prey to be caught in their webs. But other spiders, such as the desert tarantula, sit in their holes and wait for prey to pass—which they then leap onto and kill!

Scorpions usually lie in wait for prey to pass by. Then they reach out with their pincers to grab and hold the victim as they eat it. If their victim struggles, they inject a lethal dose of venom. The bark scorpion's sting can kill children and pets!

HUNTING GROUNDS

IS THAT ORCA?

   Killer whales are as big as a school bus, but heavier. They swim like lightning to catch prey with their 48 sharp, curved teeth. Like wolves, orcas are mammals that often hunt in groups, which are called PODS. Once they catch their victim, they tear it to pieces. Killer whales occasionally beach themselves to catch a seal, then drag it back into the sea.

A killer whale often eats 550 pounds (250 kg) of prey each day.

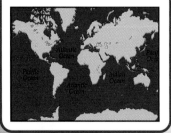

HUNTING WATERS

Atlantic Ocean

Pacific Ocean

Pacific Ocean

Indian Ocean

Atlantic Ocean

In the 1990s, these whales began to feed on sea otters in Alaska—which is not their normal prey. It's estimated that one killer whale can eat 1,825 otters per year!

 **Stats**

size: 32 feet (9.7 m) long; 8 tons (7.2 metric tons)
preferred prey: fish, seals, turtles, dolphins, sharks, other whales, penguins
attack strategy: chase and tear to pieces
works: in groups

JAWS!

Unlike whales, great white sharks are fish and they hunt alone. They're fast swimmers that can smell one drop of blood in 25 gallons (100 l) of water. So...don't scrape your knee when one is nearby!

Stats

size: up to 20 feet (11 m) long; over 2 tons (2 metric tons)
preferred prey: seals, sea lions, large fish
attack strategy: chase and tear to pieces
works: alone

When these sharks attack, they first circle their prey...sometimes bumping it to test its strength. Then they pounce. Instead of chewing their food, these sharks rip their prey into mouth-size pieces that they swallow whole.

Great white sharks have up to 3,000 jagged, triangular teeth. When they lose one tooth, another one grows in to replace it!

HUNTING WATERS

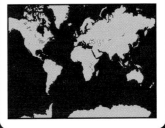

The **BALD EAGLE** is a kind of bird called a **RAPTOR**. Like all raptors, it uses its excellent vision to spot fish and other animals from high in the sky. Then it swoops down at great speed and punctures the victim's flesh with sharp **TALONS**, or claws. The dying animal is often hoisted up and carried to a rocky ledge or other safe spot, where the eagle tears and cuts the flesh with its hooked beak.

Stats

size: 10-14 pounds (4.5-6.3 kg) with a wingspan of 6-7.5 feet (1.8-2.2 m)

preferred prey: fish, but will eat almost any flesh

attack strategy: pounce and stab

works: usually alone; sometimes in pairs

Eagles can see a rabbit from about a mile (1.6km) away. Their eyesight is four times better than a human's!

BIG OR SMALL; COVERED BY HAIR, SCALES, OR SHELL; DAY HUNTERS OR NIGHT HUNTERS; ON LAND OR WATER—ALL PREDATORS HAVE ONE THING IN COMMON—THEY HUNT BECAUSE THEY'RE REALLY